2

Lost and Found

by Lana Jacobs
illustrated by MJ Illustrations

Penguin Young Readers
An Imprint of Penguin Group (USA) Inc.

The sun is out.

Strawberry Shortcake plays

with her friends.

Dear Parents and Educators,

Welcome to Penguin Young Readers! As parents and educators, you know that each child develops at his or her own pace—in terms of speech, critical thinking, and, of course, reading. Penguin Young Readers recognizes this fact. As a result, each Penguin Young Readers book is assigned a traditional easy-to-read level (1–4) as well as a Guided Reading Level (A–P). Both of these systems will help you choose the right book for your child. Please refer to the back of each book for specific leveling information. Penguin Young Readers features esteemed authors and illustrators, stories about favorite characters, fascinating nonfiction, and more!

Strawberry Shortcake™
Lost and Found

LEVEL 2
GUIDED READING LEVEL F

This book is perfect for a **Progressing Reader** who:
- can figure out unknown words by using picture and context clues;
- can recognize beginning, middle, and ending sounds;
- can make and confirm predictions about what will happen in the text; and
- can distinguish between fiction and nonfiction.

Here are some **activities** you can do during and after reading this book:
- Comprehension: Answer the following questions about the story.
  - What are Custard and Pupcake doing when Strawberry and her friends run inside to get out of the rain?
  - How does Strawberry feel when she realizes that her pets are missing?
  - What clues help Strawberry and her friends find Custard and Pupcake?
- Sight Words: Sight words are frequently used words that readers must know just by looking at them. Knowing these words helps children develop into efficient readers. As you read the story, point out the sight words listed below.

going	look	play
help	out	run

Remember, sharing the love of reading with a child is the best gift you can give!

—Bonnie Bader, EdM
Penguin Young Readers program

*Penguin Young Readers are leveled by independent reviewers applying the standards developed by Irene Fountas and Gay Su Pinnell in *Matching Books to Readers: Using Leveled Books in Guided Reading*, Heinemann, 1999.

Penguin Young Readers
Published by the Penguin Group
Penguin Group (USA) Inc., 375 Hudson Street, New York, New York 10014, USA
Penguin Group (Canada), 90 Eglinton Avenue East, Suite 700, Toronto, Ontario M4P 2Y3, Canada
(a division of Pearson Penguin Canada Inc.)
Penguin Books Ltd., 80 Strand, London WC2R 0RL, England
Penguin Group Ireland, 25 St. Stephen's Green, Dublin 2, Ireland (a division of Penguin Books Ltd.)
Penguin Group (Australia), 250 Camberwell Road, Camberwell, Victoria 3124, Australia
(a division of Pearson Australia Group Pty. Ltd.)
Penguin Books India Pvt. Ltd., 11 Community Centre, Panchsheel Park, New Delhi—110 017, India
Penguin Group (NZ), 67 Apollo Drive, Rosedale, Auckland 0632, New Zealand
(a division of Pearson New Zealand Ltd.)
Penguin Books (South Africa) (Pty.) Ltd., 24 Sturdee Avenue, Rosebank,
Johannesburg 2196, South Africa

Penguin Books Ltd., Registered Offices: 80 Strand, London WC2R 0RL, England

 Published by Penguin Young Readers, an imprint of Penguin Group (USA) Inc., 345 Hudson Street, New York, New York 10014. Manufactured in China.

ISBN 978-0-448-45546-4 10 9 8 7 6 5 4 3 2

Her pets play, too.

Pupcake is her dog.

Custard is her cat.

Look!

It is starting to rain.

The girls run inside.

It is dry inside.

Oh no!

Where are Pupcake

and Custard?

Strawberry will look for them.

Her friends want to help.

Strawberry puts on her raincoat

and rain boots.

Don't forget the umbrellas!

Strawberry and her friends

go to the shop.

Pupcake and Custard

are not at the shop.

Strawberry and her friends

go to town.

Pupcake and Custard

are not in town.

Strawberry is sad.

Will she ever find

Pupcake and Custard?

Look!

Cat and dog

paw prints!

The girls follow
the paw prints
to a flower patch.

Look!

Pupcake and Custard

are taking a nap.

Strawberry is happy.

Now it is time to go home.

The rain has stopped.

Look!

A rainbow is in the sky!

It is a happy end to the day.